CW00375457

THIS BOOK BELONGS TO

Name:	Age:

Favourite player:

2017/2018

My Predictions...   Actual...

Blues' final position:

Blues' top scorer:

Championship winners:

Championship top scorer:

FA Cup winners:

EFL Cup winners:

Contributors: Paul Leedham, Peter Rogers & Rob Mason

A TWOCAN PUBLICATION

©2017. Published by twocan under licence from Birmingham City FC.

ISBN 978-1-909872-88-2

PICTURE CREDITS: Press Association, Action Images, Roy Smiljanic.

£8.99

CONTENTS

The Squad 2017/18	6
Double Acts - Claridge & Francis	16
Che Adams Poster	18
Trevor Francis' Six Steps to Stardom	19
Championship Key Players	20
Goal of the Season	24
Jota Poster	25
Who Are Ya?	26
Training to Win	28
David Davis Poster	30
Football 50	31
The Team 2017/18	32
Player of the Season	34
What Ball?	35
Che Adams' Six Steps to Stardom	36
Harlee Dean Poster	37
Championship Challenge	38
David Stockdale Poster	42
Christophe Dugarry's Six Steps to Stardom	43
World Cup Quiz	44
Double Acts - Dann & Johnson	46
Make Your Own Foozball Team	48
Lukas Jutkiewicz Poster	49
Christmas Crackers	50
Fantastic	52
Emilio Nsue Poster	54
Made in Birmingham Nathan Redmond	55
Home Turf	56
Second Half of the Season	58
Made in Birmingham Josh Dacres-Cogley	60
Marc Roberts Poster	61
Answers	62

EMILIO NSUE

2 DEFENDER

COUNTRY: Equatorial Guinea **DOB:** 30/09/1989

A versatile player, Nsue can play either on the right side of defence or right wing. He began his professional career with RCD Mallorca in Spain and although born in Mallorca, he is an Equatorial Guinea international.

MARC ROBERTS

4 DEFENDER

COUNTRY: England **DOB:** 26/07/1990

Roberts joined Blues from Barnsley this summer on a five-year deal. A committed and determined centre-half, he captained Barnsley in their first season back in the Championship during the 2016/17 campaign, amassing 40 appearances at the heart of their backline.

JONATHAN GROUNDS

3 DEFENDER

COUNTRY: England **DOB:** 02/02/1988

Former Oldham Athletic defender, Grounds joined Blues in the summer of 2014 and has been a mainstay of the Blues defence during his first three seasons at the Club. He operates predominantly as a left-back but can also stand-in at centre-back if required.

BCFC SQUAD 2017/18

MAXIME COLIN

5 DEFENDER

COUNTRY: France **DOB:** 15/11/1991

Colin joined Blues from Brentford on 31 August 2017 on a four-year deal for an undisclosed fee. He was the third signing from the Bees in 24 hours following the transfers of Harlee Dean and Jota. He has a reputation as an energetic full-back who is good on the ball and keen to get forward.

MAIKEL KIEFTENBELD

6 MIDFIELDER

COUNTRY: Netherlands **DOB:** 26/06/1990

A dynamic central midfielder, Kieftenbeld joined Blues in July 2015 from FC Groningen. He will be hoping to reach the century mark of appearances for Blues during the 2017/18 campaign.

CRAIG GARDNER

8 MIDFIELDER

COUNTRY: England **DOB:** 25/11/1986

Gardner re-joined Blues on loan from West Bromwich Albion in January 2017, five-and-half-years after leaving the Club. This was made permanent in the summer of 2017. He was a key player in Birmingham's historic run to Carling Cup success in 2011.

ISAAC VASSELL

11 FORWARD

COUNTRY: England **DOB:** 09/09/1993

Vassell joined Blues this August from Luton Town, he spent only one full season with the Hatters but his performances marked him down as one of the game's most exciting young talents.

LUKAS JUTKIEWICZ

10 FORWARD

COUNTRY: England **DOB:** 28/03/1989

Jutkiewicz initially joined Blues on loan from Burnley in August 2010, but following a string of impressive performances the deal was made permanent in January 2017 for a fee of £1m. He finished the 2016/17 campaign as Blues' top scorer with 12 goals from his 40 appearances!

HARLEE DEAN

12 DEFENDER

COUNTRY: England **DOB:** 26/07/1991

6ft 3in Harlee Dean joined Blues on the August 2017 Deadline Day from Brentford. With the Bees since November 2011, he clocked up an impressive 249 appearances and scored ten goals. He also twice won the club's Player of the Year accolade.

CHE ADAMS

14
FORWARD

COUNTRY: England DOB: 13/07/1996

Adams can operate as an attacking midfielder or striker and penned a new five-year deal with Blues in September 2017. During his first season at St. Andrew's he made 42 appearances and scored seven goals, including the crucial final-day winner at Bristol City which kept Blues in the Championship.

DAVID STOCKDALE

13
GOALKEEPER

COUNTRY: England DOB: 20/09/1985

Stockdale was one of the most consistent players in the Sky Bet Championship last season as he helped the Seagulls to promotion. His performances saw him voted into the PFA Championship Team of the Year, as well as being included in the EFL Championship 2016/17 Team of the Season!

COHEN BRAMALL

15
DEFENDER

COUNTRY: England DOB: 02/04/1996

Blues snapped up Bramall on a season-long loan from Arsenal in August 2017. A left-back who has pace in abundance, he has broken into the Gunners first team squad.

CHEIKH NDOYE 17
MIDFIELDER

COUNTRY: Senegal **DOB:** 29/03/1986

Blues beat a number of clubs to sign experienced Senegalese international, Ndoye, on 14 July 2017. He is strong in the air and can break up play as well as dictate tempo forcefully.

SAM GALLAGHER 18
FORWARD

COUNTRY: England **DOB:** 15/09/1995

Blues beat off strong competition to secure 6ft 4in striker Gallagher on a season-long loan from Southampton. He represented Scotland at Under-19 level before switching to England in 2014.

JACQUES MAGHOMA 19
MIDFIELDER

COUNTRY: Congo DR **DOB:** 23/10/1987

Maghoma joined Blues in June 2015 from Sheffield Wednesday. He is a powerful ball-playing midfielder, who can operate on either flank or off the front. Although born in Zaire, he is a full Democratic Republic of Congo international.

JEREMIE BOGA

20
MIDFIELDER

COUNTRY: Côte D'Ivoire   DOB: 03/01/1997

An exciting Ivory Coast international, Boga came through the ranks at Chelsea and joined Blues on a season-long loan in August 2017. His skilful, agile dribbling and ability to go past people make him an impressive performer.

JASON LOWE

21
MIDFIELDER

COUNTRY: England   DOB: 02/09/1991

Blues completed the signing of Lowe on a one-year contract on the final day of the summer 2017 transfer window. An ex-England Under-21 international, he predominantly plays as a holding midfielder but has also featured at right-back.

CARL JENKINSON

22
DEFENDER

COUNTRY: England   DOB: 08/02/1992

An athletic right-back who can also play in central defence, Jenkinson joined on loan this season from Arsenal. He helped Arsenal to the 2014 FA Cup triumph before spending two successful seasons on loan at West Ham United, making 59 appearances for the Hammers.

DAVID COTTERILL

23
MIDFIELDER

COUNTRY: Wales **DOB:** 04/12/1987

A Wales international, Cotterill made the switch to Blues ahead of the 2014/15 campaign. He surpassed the 100-appearance mark for Blues midway through the 2016/17 season!

LIAM WALSH

24
MIDFIELDER

COUNTRY: England **DOB:** 15/09/1997

Everton's Liam Walsh joined Blues on loan on the final day of the summer 2017 transfer window. He is a ball-playing central midfielder by trade who is comfortable in possession and boasts a wide range of passing.

JOSH DACRES-COGLEY

25
DEFENDER

COUNTRY: England **DOB:** 12/03/1996

Dacres-Cogley is a product of the Club's academy system having joined Blues back in 2011. He made his first team bow in the EFL Cup against Oxford United in August 2016 and went on to make 17 appearances last season.

DAVID DAVIS

26
MIDFIELDER

COUNTRY: England **DOB:** 20/02/1991

Davis' impressive performances during the 2016/17 campaign saw him recognised as the Supporters' Player of the Year and Players' Player of the Season! Midway through that season, he also penned a new deal to tie him to the Club until the summer of 2020.

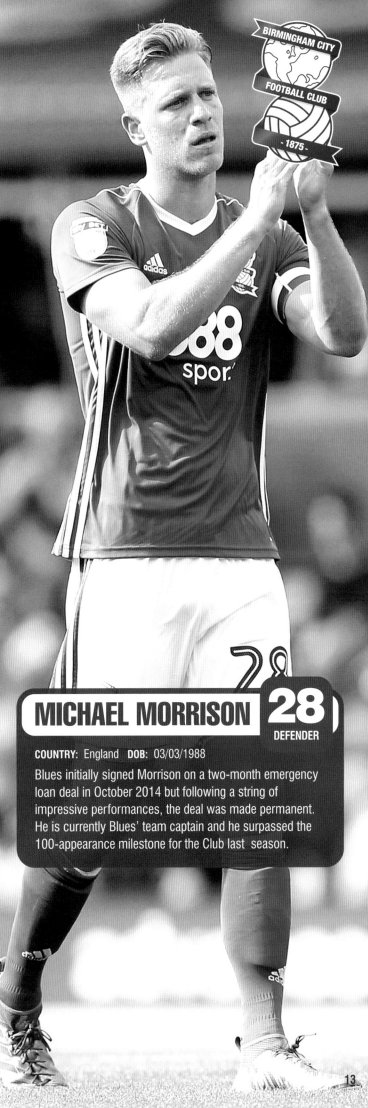

JOTA 27
MIDFIELDER

COUNTRY: Spain DOB: 16/06/1991

Spanish winger Jota became Blues' record signing when he joined on 31 August 2017 from Brentford. Birmingham City fought off intense competition to land the talented playmaker on a four-year deal for a fee in excess of £6m.

MICHAEL MORRISON 28
DEFENDER

COUNTRY: England DOB: 03/03/1988

Blues initially signed Morrison on a two-month emergency loan deal in October 2014 but following a string of impressive performances, the deal was made permanent. He is currently Blues' team captain and he surpassed the 100-appearance milestone for the Club last season.

TOMASZ KUSZCZAK | 29
GOALKEEPER

COUNTRY: Poland **DOB:** 20/03/1982

An experienced stopper and former Polish international, Kuszczak joined Blues in July 2015 and made 42 appearances in his first season at the Club. In May 2017, he penned a new three-year deal with Blues.

COREY O'KEEFFE | 30
MIDFIELDER

COUNTRY: Republic of Ireland **DOB:** 05/06/1998

Birmingham-born O'Keeffe is an athletic and versatile player. His drive, determination and leadership qualities along with his ability saw him rewarded with a first team squad number in December 2016.

PAUL ROBINSON | 40
DEFENDER

COUNTRY: England **DOB:** 17/12/1978

A former England Under-21 international, Robinson has clocked up over 170 appearances during his time at St. Andrew's and penned a new one-year deal in the summer of 2017.

NICOLAI BROCK-MADSEN
44
FORWARD

COUNTRY: Denmark   DOB: 09/01/1993

A Danish international, Brock-Madsen joined Blues in August 2015 on a four-year deal. He gained valuable experience on a season-long loan with Dutch top-flight side PEC Zwolle in 2016/17 and enjoyed a successful time at the Eredivisie club, scoring 11 goals in 26 appearances.

WES HARDING
45
DEFENDER

COUNTRY: England   DOB: 20/10/1996

A central defender, Harding is now in his fifth season at the Club having joined the Academy in 2012, he wore the captain's armband for the Under-23s on numerous occasions in 2016/17, during which he chalked up 20 competitive games.

STEPHEN GLEESON
50
MIDFIELDER

COUNTRY: Republic of Ireland   DOB: 03/08/1988

A former MK Dons midfielder and Republic of Ireland international, Gleeson joined Blues in June 2014. He made his Blues debut in the 2014/15 opening-day defeat at Boro and is another member of the 100 appearances club at Blues.

Birmingham City ensured a swift return to the second tier of English football in 1994/95 as strikers Steve Claridge and Kevin Francis spearheaded a double success of promotion and Wembley glory.

DOUBLE

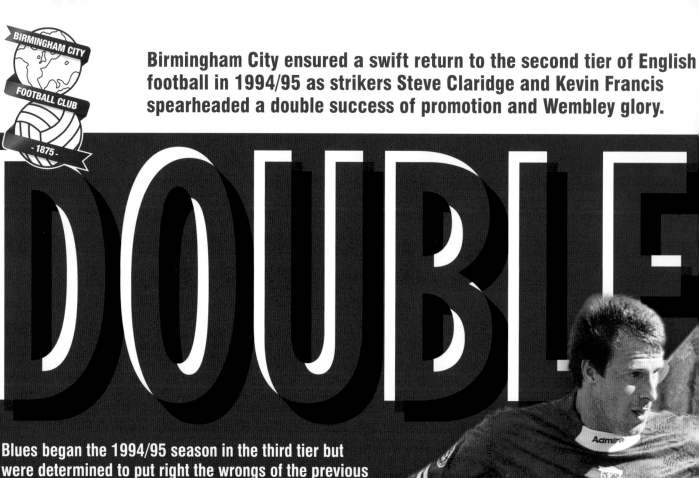

Blues began the 1994/95 season in the third tier but were determined to put right the wrongs of the previous campaign which had seen them suffer relegation under the management of Barry Fry. Despite the disappointment of slipping down a division, Fry remained in charge and the goals of Claridge and Francis gave Blues fans a season to remember.

Claridge had been brought to St. Andrew's by Fry in a £350,000 deal from Cambridge United in January 1994 but his arrival was unable to prevent relegation. However, he certainly proved his worth with 25 goals in all competitions in 1994/95 as he became the first Blues player since Trevor Francis to score 20 league goals in a season.

The team had progressed up the table and into the automatic promotion places by the turn of the year and at that stage Fry opted to enhance his striking options with the £800,000 signing of giant Stockport County striker Kevin Francis who had netted an impressive 88 goals in 152 league games while at Edgeley Park.

CLARIDGE

Birmingham-born Francis jumped at the chance of playing for his home city club and his giant six ft, seven in frame, coupled with the natural goalscoring instincts of Claridge were seen by Fry as the perfect goalscoring double act to see the Club to promotion and so it proved.

ACTS

After sealing his January move, Francis wasted little time in joining Claridge among the goals and netted his first two league goals for the Club in a 4-2 St. Andrew's success over York City. He managed an impressive five goals in three games as Blues held off their fellow promotion challengers. Claridge and Francis were both on the scoresheet as Blues defeated Oxford United 3-0 at St. Andrew's in March.

A highly successful season for the Club ended with promotion as champions and Wembley glory in the Football League Trophy. Claridge and Francis were once again paired together for the Wembley showpiece against Carlisle United but it was Paul Tait who stole the headlines with the 'Golden Goal' that sealed victory.

Claridge ended the campaign with 25 goals from his 57 outings in all competitions while Francis scored nine goals from 18 games following his January arrival. In January 1996, Claridge made a big money move to Leicester City, Francis meanwhile remained at Birmingham until 1998 when he joined Oxford United and both players are fondly remember for their combined efforts in Blues' double winning season.

Manager Barry Fry celebrates with Kevin Francis

& FRANCIS

CHE
ADAMS
14

CONSIDERED THE GREATEST BLUES PLAYER OF ALL TIME, HERE ARE SIX FACTS BEHIND TREVOR FRANCIS' POPULARITY WITH ALL AT ST. ANDREW'S...

1. ENTERING THE RECORD BOOKS

Trevor Francis wrote his name in the Birmingham City record books when he played the first of his 329 games for the Club. Francis became the Club's youngest ever player when he made his debut against Cardiff City on 5 September 1970. He was aged just 16 years 139 days old when he featured in a Second Division match at Ninian Park. A week later he marked his home debut with the only goal of the game to seal a victory over Oxford United.

2. PROMOTION HERO

Francis helped inspire Blues to promotion to the First Division in 1971/72 as he netted 12 league goals in 39 appearances for Freddie Goodwin's side. He scored crucial goals in the promotion run-in as Blues sealed vital victories over Blackpool, Hull City and Sheffield Wednesday. Promotion was finally secured on the final day of the campaign as Blues ended the season runners-up to Norwich City.

3. GOALS, GOALS, GOALS

Blues' 1976/77 First Division campaign saw Francis end an ever-present season as leading goalscorer with 21 First Division goals to his name. Among those 21 top-flight strikes was a remarkable goal against Queens Park Rangers that saw him collect the ball almost on the touchline and sidestep a series of defenders before delivering a blistering drive past the Rangers 'keeper at the Railway End.

4. AN ENGLAND INTERNATIONAL

Such was Francis' superb form at club level, international recognition duly arrived. On Wednesday 9 February 1977 Francis won his first England cap in an International Friendly at Wembley. England slipped to a 2-0 home defeat to a Holland side that included Dutch legends Johan Neeskens and Johan Cruyff. Francis would go on to win a total of 52 caps for his country.

5. THE MILLION POUND MAN

After gaining England recognition Francis was very much a man in demand. So much so that in February 1979 reigning First Division champions Nottingham Forest paid a transfer fee of £1m for his services. This was the first time a player had ever been sold between two English clubs for a seven figure sum.

6. RETURNING HERO

Following a long and successful playing career plus a stint managing Sheffield Wednesday, Francis returned to his spiritual home of St. Andrew's as Blues manager in 1996. His greatest achievement as boss was leading the team to the 2000/01 League Cup final where they faced the mighty Liverpool. Despite tackling opposition from a division higher, Blues pushed their illustrious opponents all the way at Cardiff's Millennium Stadium only to be bravely defeated in a penalty shoot-out.

TREVOR FRANCIS'

SIX STEPS TO STARDOM

ALEX SMITHIES
QPR

Now 27, former England U19 international Smithies, was at one time rated as one of the country's hottest young goalkeepers after breaking into Huddersfield Town's first eleven when just 17. Despite a lot of interest, he stayed with the West Yorkshire side, playing 274 games for the Terriers until his 2015 move to the capital.

KEIREN WESTWOOD
SHEFFIELD WEDNESDAY

Westwood's excellent displays between the sticks have been rewarded with over 20 international caps for the Republic of Ireland. The excellent shot-stopper has made over 130 appearances each for Sheffield Wednesday, Coventry City and Carlisle United as well as being honoured with the Player of the Year award at each club!

ADAM DAVIES
BARNSLEY

Although Davies was born in Germany, the 25-year-old comes from a Welsh family and although he's yet to debut, he has been a part of several Wales squads. After starting his career at Everton followed by a spell with Sheffield Wednesday, Davies is now a real safe pair of hands for the Tykes with over 100 appearances behind him.

goalkeepers

The value of a great goalkeeper just can't be underestimated. We've selected six top stoppers who will look to shine over the coming months.

FELIX WIEDWALD
LEEDS UNITED

After making the move to Yorkshire from Werder Bremen in the summer, former Germany U20 international Wiedwald really caught the eye and did so well that he was chosen ahead of Leeds United's ex-England 'keeper Rob Green. The imposing 6ft 3in goalie has also played in Germany with MSV Duisburg and Eintracht Frankfurt.

SCOTT CARSON
DERBY COUNTY

The former England goalkeeper is still one of the best 'keepers around. Carson commands his penalty area and has a real presence on the pitch. After starting out with a handful of appearances for both Leeds United and Liverpool, he has now played over 400 career games both in England and Turkey.

VITO MANNONE
READING

Mannone came to England from Atalanta and continued his career at Arsenal. Following loan spells with Barnsley and Hull City, he moved North to Sunderland where he was the hero of the Black Cats' run to the 2014 League Cup final, starring in their semi-final shoot-out win against Manchester United at Old Trafford. Player of the Year at the Stadium of Light that year, Mannone moved to the Madejski Stadium last summer.

MICHAEL DAWSON
HULL CITY

Former England and Spurs centre-back, Dawson made his name with Nottingham Forest before moving to the capital in 2005. The commanding defender has been voted Player of the Year with both Tottenham and the Tigers as well as winning the League Cup with Spurs a decade ago. The City skipper's consistant displays have seen him selected for the PFA Team of the Year at both ends of his career, in 2003 and 2016.

HARLEE DEAN
BIRMINGHAM CITY

Dean arrived at St. Andrew's towards the end of the summer 2017 transfer window from Brentford. He had been with the Bees since 2011 and while at Griffin Park, the imposing 6ft 3in central-defender's passion and commitment to the cause helped him clock up 249 appearances, hit the back of the net ten times and pick up the club's Player of the Year award twice. Dean's whole-hearted approach to the game will make him a popular figure with teammates and fans alike.

RYAN SESSEGNON
FULHAM

Probably the best young player in the Championship, London-born Sessegnon is the cousin of the former Sunderland and WBA, Benin international Stephane Sessegnon. He debuted for Fulham in August 2016 when he was only 16. Despite playing at left-back, he was joint top scorer at the 2017 European U19 tournament won with England.

defenders

Protecting a lead, battling for that all important clean sheet and trying to help support their attack-minded teammates - here are six top quality Championship defenders to look out for.

SOULEYMANE BAMBA
CARDIFF CITY

Experienced Ivory Coast international centre-back Bamba was born in France and began his playing career with Paris Saint-Germain before a move to Dunfermline. After plying his trade in Scotland, England, Turkey and Italy, he made Wales the sixth country he has called home when he signed for Neil Warnock's Bluebirds.

JOHN EGAN
BRENTFORD

The Republic of Ireland international centre-back has the happy knack of chipping in with his share of goals. He is a proper centre-back, a leader with a real hunger to keep the ball out of the net. Egan's dad was a famous Gaelic footballer while his mother has a League of Ireland winners medal with Cork Rangers, so it's no surprise he is a talented lad destined for the top.

NATHAN BAKER
BRISTOL CITY

After 13 years and over 100 games for Aston Villa, former England U21 international left-footed centre-back Nathan Baker signed for the Robins last summer after spending the previous season on loan at Ashton Gate. Brave and committed, Villa's loss is certainly Bristol's gain.

CHEIKH NDOYE
BIRMINGHAM CITY

A commanding 6ft 3in powerhouse in the centre of midfield, Senegal international Ndoye moved to St. Andrew's in 2017 from French club Angers who he skippered in last season's Coupe de France final, narrowly losing 1-0 to all conquering Paris Saint-Germain. He previously played for Creteil with whom he won the Championnat National (the third division of the French football) in 2013.

AIDEN McGEADY
SUNDERLAND

With almost 100 caps for the Republic of Ireland, McGeady is one of the most magical wingers in the Championship. In 2010 he commanded a fee of almost £10m when joining Spartak Moscow from Celtic with whom he had won seven trophies. He arrived at the Stadium of Light from Everton after playing for Black Cats boss Simon Grayson last season on loan to Preston.

DANIEL JOHNSON
PRESTON NORTH END

Originally from Kingston, Jamaica, Johnson is unmistakable with his very long hair and equally unmistakable with the energy he shows all over the pitch. He progressed through the Aston Villa academy and went on a trio of loans before Preston signed him in January 2015. Eight goals in midfield from 23 games that season helped power Preston to promotion.

midfielders

The Championship is packed with top-class midfield performers - we've chosen six midfield maestros who could well be real star turns for their respective clubs this season.

NATHAN THOMAS
SHEFFIELD UNITED

A talented and exciting winger, Thomas made the jump from, just relegated from League Two Hartlepool, to just promoted from League One Sheffield United and got off to a flying start with a debut goal in a League Cup win over Walsall. He likes to score the spectacular, finding the back of the net nine times for struggling Hartlepool last season and it's only a matter of time until Thomas is a fans' favourite at Bramall Lane.

RUBEN NEVES
WOLVES

Wanderers' Portuguese international record-signing midfielder from Porto cost a reported £15.0m in 2017. Neves is just 20, but reads the game like a seasoned professional and seems destined for the top. Wolves hope this natural leader will guide them to the Premier League. He is also the youngest player to captain a team in the Champions League, Porto at the age of 18.

JEM KARACAN
BOLTON WANDERERS

Karacan is at his best when he's hassling and disrupting the opposition's midfield with his typically high-energy performance. London -born to an English mother and Turkish father, Karacan has played for Turkey at junior levels and been in full international squads, but has yet to make his full international debut. He has played club football in Turkey as well as England and after starting over 150 games for Reading he joined Bolton from Galatasary in 2017.

CHAMPIONSHIP KEY PLAYERS

MARVIN SORDELL
BURTON ALBION

Still only 26, Sordell seems to have been around for a long time. He represented Great Britain at the 2012 London Olympics and has also played for England at U21 level. He made his name with Watford and once commanded a big money move into the Premier League with Bolton. He is a consistent and versatile performer who likes to shoot from distance.

DARYL MURPHY
NOTTINGHAM FOREST

The Republic of Ireland international was the Championship's top scorer in 2014/15 with Ipswich Town when the targetman's power and pace also earned him the Tractor Boys' Player of the Year award. He won Premier League promotion with Newcastle United last season and Sunderland in 2007 and also had a spell with Celtic in the SPL at the start of the decade.

STEVE MORISON
MILLWALL

33-year-old Morison is a Lions legend. He is now in his third spell with the club and is the reigning Millwall Player of the Year. The towering striker has scored over 230 goals in a career that started in 2001 with Northampton Town and has seen him play for England at 'C' level (non-league), before becoming a full international with Wales.

forwards

Goals win games and when it comes to finding the back of the net at Championship level they don't come much sharper than these six great goal getters.

BRITT ASSOMBALONGA
MIDDLESBROUGH

Assombalonga is arguably the best striker outside the Premier League. He is a proven goalscorer in the Championship, scoring 30 goals in 47 league starts for Forest. The Teessiders invested £15m to bring in the son of a former Zaire international and if he stays injury-free, could fire Boro back into the Premier League.

NELSON OLIVEIRA
NORWICH CITY

The Portugal international is a threatening striker, quick off the mark with first-class technique and neat footwork. Oliveira, who started with Benfica, had six loans with clubs in Portugal, France, England and Wales, before committing his future to the Carrow Road club in 2016. He scored 15 times in 31 games in his first season as a Canary and commenced the current campaign with three goals in his first three matches.

MARTYN WAGHORN
IPSWICH TOWN

The former England U21 international returned to the English league last summer after two years in Scotland with Rangers where he won a Player of the Year award to go with the Young Player of the Year trophy he won with Leicester. Waghorn has the ability to play anywhere across the front four and his good scoring record continued this season with four goals in his first three Championship games.

GOAL OF THE SEASON

Kerim Frei

Rotherham United 1 Birmingham City 1

Sky Bet Championship, New York Stadium, Friday 14 April 2017

Kerim Frei's stay at Blues may have been largely short and uneventful, but the Turkish international will forever have a place in the Club's record books after his strike against Rotherham United earned him the Goal of the Season accolade at the end of the 2016/17 campaign.

Frei had joined Blues from Turkish champions Besiktas in January 2017, having been brought in by former manager Gianfranco Zola on a three-and-a-half-year deal.

The winger initially struggled to find his feet with Blues in the Championship and most of his appearances came off the substitutes' bench.

But it was in his 12th and penultimate game for the Club away at Rotherham United on Friday 14 April 2017, that Frei scored his one and only goal in royal blue, which was also voted as the best scored by a Blues player that season.

Blues headed up to their match against their South Yorkshire opponents desperately in search of points to try and maintain their Championship survival.

After a dour first 45, which brought just three shots on target, Blues started the second-half as poorly as they had played the first. And when Rotherham started to get the upper hand, former boss Gianfranco Zola elected to change his system and brought on Frei in place of defender Paul Robinson.

Frei soon began to make an impact with his pace and won a succession of free-kicks for the visitors, which were ultimately squandered by Craig Gardner and Lukas Jutkiewicz.

Then with 17 minutes to go, Che Adams won a deserved free-kick in a central position five yards outside the D.

This time it was Frei who took on the free-kick duties, and the 2,600 travelling Blues fans in the stadium were glad he did as he stepped and curled a peach of a strike into the top corner of the net leaving Millers goalkeeper Richard O'Donnell floundering and sparking scenes of jubilation amongst him and his colleagues.

But with Blues desperately looking to cling on they suffered a blow as they conceded an equalising goal with just five minutes remaining and were forced to settle for a crucial point on their travels.

27

JOTA

Can you identify...

...all of these Blues stars?

WHO ARE YA

8
9
10

TRAINING TO WIN

Footballers are finely-tuned athletes with impressive skills which they need to demonstrate under pressure. They have to be physically and mentally strong.

The world's top sports stars face tough challenges in their chosen field, but they can be very different to those that a footballer has to face. In sports such as golf, athletics and even tennis or a team game like cricket, you have no-one physically trying to stop you when you're attempting to play the game.

However, think about what you have to do as a footballer. You have to have the ability to control the ball, even when it comes to you at speed or a difficult angle. You have to be able to pass over short and long distances. You have to be able to head the ball. Not every player can do it all, but at least some members of the team have to be able to shoot well and tackle too.

All this would be hard enough without having your opponent doing their utmost to stop you - holding you, pushing you, knocking you off balance and quite possibly fouling you. So a footballer has to have strength and speed as well as skill.

To become a professional footballer, firstly, you have to have bundles of skill which you've probably spent all your life developing, but you also have to be extremely fit. Footballers do all kinds of exercises to get fit, and stay fit. They work in the gym to build up their strength and they also work with fitness coaches who keep them in peak physical condition.

They have to be very careful to follow a healthy diet. If they don't, it makes it hard for them to stay match fit. They avoid foods with lots of fat, so they rarely eat things like crisps, chocolate, chips and burgers, if at all.

Once they have reached full fitness for the start of the season, footballers usually train for about two hours a day, four or five days a week if they have one game a week. It is important that they also rest at the right times or they won't feel at their best during games. Some players will also do other exercises like pilates or yoga to help them stay supple.

There is a lot to being a professional footballer. Staying in peak condition requires a lot of dedication and players who look after themselves well by eating healthily and training hard will be able to give their team 100% on the pitch.

26

DAVID
DAVIS

FOOTBALL 50

Here is a list of 50 footie words. All but one are hidden in the grid, can you work out which is missing?

BIRMINGHAM CITY
FOOTBALL CLUB
- 1875 -

```
S U B S T I T U T E I S R E D L E I F D I M
M A A Z P L E A O S U J J Y O Y T N D T R K O
A Q E X T R A T I M E R L C K J A U D I M E
N B L C A C A D E M Y K F Y U K O B C B N P
O N I E S A J W R T P E X R T G D K H B P B
F R F J A P H I A E M R Y C U C O C A L T L
T H I W Y T D B K W S T O D Y F B R L I E I
H D N E P A R X J B I S C M F A U O L N E T
E D A Z L I N E S M A N I T O F D G E G H R
M B L D S N W A E C Q I U N A T P U N Q S A
A I W Y H C O R N E R F L A G O I M G Z N N
T E H E A D E R V L H Y S R I R C O E R A S
C B I M J E E L U R E D I S F F O K N V E F
H G S G Q F P R N U A L K L G I H O B M L E
F R T U F E L N B T F E R E G A N A M A C R
M E L K E N G F B Y D H T D A F V G O H J W
Y K E F C D R P O C M F H L H J W G A B H I
S I O W O E K S P U I A O A V S N F D M I N
A R W M N R Q N R P L H T U O E M S R T J D
O T K C I K E E R F Y T D C D J Y B A G T O
G S O V T C A D T B R X N L H S F A C U P W
K A M P Q E T I C I E F O M R N G E W B S U
C I A M S K M R C A S G C G O U K O O C E M
I Y E J A E R K D I R F H S R E Y A L P V C
K C T E P D R G B F K D A E U G A E L E R S
R E T L T N W T J N G E Q U A L I S E R E H
O Y S P A I A W N G S R C V S F G L Y F S R
S S R N T N H L H E L S U N U T M E G U E N
S K I J S J E V R L C W A S P O L S O F R J
I K F P F H M P L K U F E H E L A O E T I M
C R O S S B A R S C T T M R O J I R W T Q N
S O I R M E X I C A N W A V E P E O L D K P
G A S U N N A E R T U B R E P E E K L A O G
```

Academy
Captain
Centre Spot
Challenge
Clean Sheet
Corner Flag
Crossbar
Defender
Derby Match
Dressing Room
Dribbling
Dugout
Equaliser
Extra Time
FA Cup
Fans
Final Whistle
First Team
Fixture
Foul
Free Kick
Goalkeeper
Golden Goal
Half Time
Hat-trick
Header
Injury Time
Kick-off
League
Linesman
Manager
Man of the Match
Mexican Wave
Midfielder
Nutmeg
Offside Rule
Penalty
Players
Pre-season
Promotion
Red Card
Referee
Reserves
Scissor Kick
Striker
Substitute
Tackle
Transfer Window
Volley
Yellow Card

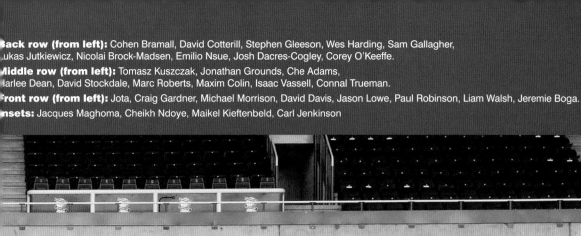

Back row (from left): Cohen Bramall, David Cotterill, Stephen Gleeson, Wes Harding, Sam Gallagher, Lukas Jutkiewicz, Nicolai Brock-Madsen, Emilio Nsue, Josh Dacres-Cogley, Corey O'Keeffe.

Middle row (from left): Tomasz Kuszczak, Jonathan Grounds, Che Adams, Harlee Dean, David Stockdale, Marc Roberts, Maxim Colin, Isaac Vassell, Connal Trueman.

Front row (from left): Jota, Craig Gardner, Michael Morrison, David Davis, Jason Lowe, Paul Robinson, Liam Walsh, Jeremie Boga.

Insets: Jacques Maghoma, Cheikh Ndoye, Maikel Kieftenbeld, Carl Jenkinson

PLAYER OF THE SEASON

David Davis

During what was very much a season of transition both on and off the pitch, one of the main constants was dynamic midfielder David Davis out in the centre of the park.

Since joining the Club from Wolves in August 2014, the Smethwick-born midfielder has become an increasingly popular member of the squad amongst the Blues faithful for the energy and commitment he demonstrates every time be pulls on the royal blue shirt.

The 2016/17 campaign saw the 26-year-old play in a variety of midfield positions during his 42 appearances. Whether he was shielding the defence, playing further forwards in a more attacking role, or even on occasion on the wing, Davis never let the side down.

And as well as his general all-round play and tenacity, there was also the small matter of his success in local derbies.

In the home game against Birmingham rivals Aston Villa, he scored a second-half equaliser in a 1-1 draw, and against former club Wolves he was also on target in the 2-1 success at Molineux.

In what is a measure of the man and his importance to the side, as well a winning the Supporters' Player of the Season, Davis was also recognised by his team-mates as he also collected the Players' Player of the Season.

And to quote Davis himself on being recognised: "I am massively proud.

"I think my game has developed, working under the three managers I have this season each has taught me something different and pointed out different weaknesses they have seen in me.

"I have tried to work on those, obviously I can't perfect it in one game or two games but I would like to think I paid enough attention to correc it in some aspects of my game.

"The positive feedback means the world to be honest because I haven't come through this academy, I have come from a rival team. I could have easily been tarnished a certain way.

"But the fans have taken to me like I am one of their own and I have just tried to give 110 per cent because I know that's what Birmingham City fans like."

There are too many footballs!

WHATBALL?

Work out which is the real ball in each photo.

CHE ADAMS ONLY ARRIVED AT ST. ANDREW'S IN 2016 BUT IS ALREADY A FANS' FAVOURITE. HERE ARE SIX FACTORS BEHIND THE ATTACKING MIDFIELDER'S POPULARITY...

1. CHOOSING BLUES

Adams' impressive form at Sheffield United had won him a host of admirers, in fact the majority of Championship clubs had been alerted to his qualities and sent scouts to monitor his progress at Bramall Lane. After a summer of intense transfer speculation surrounding the youngster, it was Blues who won the battle for his signature in August 2016.

2. ON THE SCORESHEET

The all-action attacker wasted little time in showing the St. Andrew's faithful just what he was all about. After making his debut as a second-half substitute in a 1-1 draw away to Wigan Athletic, his home debut came when he was named in the starting line-up for a Midlands derby with Wolves. Adams opened the scoring after 24 minutes to give the side a lead they held at the interval. A below par second-half display from Blues resulted in a 3-1 defeat on an afternoon when Adams' debut was very much the positive aspect from a disappointing result.

3. SALVAGING A POINT

Following his summer switch from the Blades, Adams was clearly enjoying life at St. Andrew's as Blues continued to climb the Championship table in the first half of the 2016/17 campaign. Adams registered his second goal for the Club at home to Preston North End in September. With Blues 2-1 down at the break, his second-half goal secured a secured a valuable point from a 2-2 draw.

4. WINNING GOAL

Adams scored his first winning goal for Blues as they took maximum points from their 19 November meeting with Bristol City at St. Andrew's. The match looked all set to end in a goalless stalemate until Adams struck the only goal of the game nine minutes from time to secure a fifth home win of the season of Gary Rowett's side.

5. MR CONSISTENT

Despite a dramatic campaign at St. Andrew's that saw Adams serve three different managers during his debut season with the Club, he clearly impressed all of them. A consistent name in the Blues starting line under Gary Rowett, Gianfranco Zola and Harry Redknapp, Adams played a total of 42 games for Blues in 2016/17 and ended the season with seven goals to his name.

6. VITAL STRIKE

Adams wrote his name into Birmingham City folklore on the final day of the 2016/17 campaign as he scored the goal that preserved the Club's Championship status. After having his red card against Huddersfield Town in the previous game overturned, Adams started Blues' must-win match away to Bristol City and scored the game's only goal after 16 minutes to trigger a wonderful staying up party!

CHE ADAMS'
SIX STEPS TO STARDOM

HARLEE
DEAN

12

CHAMPIONSHIP

ASTON VILLA

Which England and Chelsea legend did Aston Villa sign at the start of this season?

1 answer

Aston Villa won the European Cup in 1981. Did they beat Bayern Munich, Barcelona or Real Madrid in the final?

2 answer

Who is the former Sunderland manager who started the season as Villa manager?

3 answer

BARNSLEY

During the summer Barnsley signed Ezekiel Fryers from which Premier League London club?

5 answer

Who is Barnsley's captain?

4 answer

Who is the Tykes' manager?

6 answer

BIRMINGHAM CITY

When did Birmingham City last win the League Cup?

8 answer

Blues completed a record signing on transfer deadline day, summer 2017, who was it?

9 answer

Who scored Blues' first league goal this season?

7 answer

BOLTON WANDERERS

How many times have Bolton won the FA Cup?

10 answer

Bolton reached the League Cup final in 2004 but lost to which club who are also now in the Championship?

11 answer

Name the manager who led Bolton to promotion in 2017 in his first season at the club.

12 answer

BRENTFORD

Brentford are West London rivals of QPR who they knocked out of this season's Carabao Cup away from home. Did they win 3-1, 4-1 or 5-1?

13 answer

Who is Brentford's Number 9 striker this season?

14 answer

Who was the manager of Brentford from 2013 to 2015 who went on to manage Rangers and Nottingham Forest?

15 answer

BRISTOL CITY

Which Premier League team did City knock out of the Carabao Cup away from home in the second round this season?

17 answer

Who was Bristol City's Player of the Season in 2016/17?

16 answer

Who scored 23 times for Bristol City last season on loan from Chelsea?

18 answer

CHALLENGE

BURTON ALBION

Who was Burton's first summer signing ahead of the 2017/18 season?

20

Which former England international began the season as Burton's manager?

19

Which former Liverpool and Villa player signed for Burton at the start of the season?

21

CARDIFF CITY

Cardiff City are the Bluebirds but what colour were their shirts between 2012 and 2015?

22

Who was the manager who inspired Cardiff to maximum points from their first four league games of this season?

23

Who was the Chile international midfielder who moved from Cardiff to Inter Milan in 2014 and stayed with the Italian giants until 2017?

24

DERBY COUNTY

Which Derby player scored the opening goal at the Stadium of Light this season?

25

In what year did Derby win the FA Cup?

26

Who is the former England international Derby re-signed for a second spell at the club at the start of this season?

27

FULHAM

Who is Fulham's No 1 this season?

29

Which Spanish side beat Fulham in the final of the 2010 Europa League?

28

Who is Fulham's No 10 and their captain this season?

30

HULL CITY

Which country did Leonid Slutsky manage before taking over at Hull?

32

What is Hull's nickname?

31

Hull reached the FA Cup final in 2014 but lost to which London club?

33

IPSWICH TOWN

Who scored Town's first league goal this season?

34

Ipswich went from the third division to top flight champions in six years under the manager who later won the World Cup for England. Who was that?

35

In which season did the Tractor Boys win the FA Cup?

36

LEEDS UNITED

What is Leeds United's club anthem?

37 answer

Between 1965 and 1974 how many times did Leeds finish in the top two of the league?

38 answer

Who is captaining the Whites this season?

39 answer

MIDDLESBROUGH

Which Spanish team beat Middlesbrough in the 2006 Europa League final?

41 answer

Who did Boro sign on a season-long loan from Swansea City in July 2017?

40 answer

Which major trophy did Boro win in 2004?

42 answer

MILLWALL

Who did Millwall play in the 2004 FA Cup final?

44 answer

Millwall began this season with one of their former Players of the Year as manager. Who?

43 answer

What is Millwall's nickname?

45 answer

NORWICH CITY

Which team did Head Coach, Daniel Farke, manage before joining City this season?

46 answer

How many League Cup finals have Norwich played in, two, three or four?

47 answer

Who is the Canaries' No 1 this season?

48 answer

NOTTINGHAM FOREST

Which Premier League club did Forest defeat away from home in the Carabao Cup in August 2017?

49 answer

Forest have twice won the European Cup (now the Champions League). True or false?

50 answer

Who is the former Brighton, Leeds and Sunderland midfielder Forest signed in August 2017?

51 answer

PRESTON NORTH END

Who was the future Everton and Manchester United manager who won the Division Two title with Preston in 2000?

53 answer

Who was Preston's top scorer last season?

52 answer

Preston did it first in 1996, Wolves equalled it in 1900 and Burnley, Sheffield United and Portsmouth have done it since. What is the feat these five clubs have achieved?

54 answer

CHALLENGE

Let's see how well you know Blues and their Championship rivals...

QUEENS PARK RANGERS

Which defender did Rangers pay a club record £12.5m for in 2013 only to sell him later that year?

56

Who is QPR's captain this season?

55

Which of the following managers have not managed QPR: Harry Redknapp, Mark Hughes, Martin O'Neill and Ian Holloway?

57

READING

Which former Manchester United defender was manager of Reading at the start of the season?

58

What position in the Championship did Reading finish in last season?

59

Who did Reading sign from Sunderland during the summer?

60

SHEFFIELD UNITED

Who is the Blades' No 9 striker this season?

61

How many points did Sheffield United earn in winning League One last season: 95, 100 or 105?

62

Goalkeeper Jamal Blackman is on a season long loan to Sheffield United from which Premier League London club?

63

SHEFFIELD WEDNESDAY

Sheffield Wednesday are one of the oldest clubs in the world. In 2017 they celebrated a major anniversary. How many years old were the club in 2017?

65

Who was Sheffield Wednesday's first 2017 summer signing?

64

Adding together Sheffield Wednesday's top flight league titles, FA Cup and League Cup wins, how many major trophies have they won: 6, 7 or 8?

66

SUNDERLAND

How many other current Championship clubs have Sunderland met in FA Cup finals?

68

Who did Sunderland sign from West Brom on the August 2017 transfer deadline day?

67

Which two academy produced players scored their first goals for the club in August 2017?

69

WOLVERHAMPTON WANDERERS

Who were last season's League Cup finalists who Wolves knocked out of this season's Carabao Cup in August?

70

Between 1950 and 1960 how many times did Wolves finish in the top two of the top flight?

71

Who is the Portuguese midfielder Wolves paid almost £16m for in the summer of 2017?

72

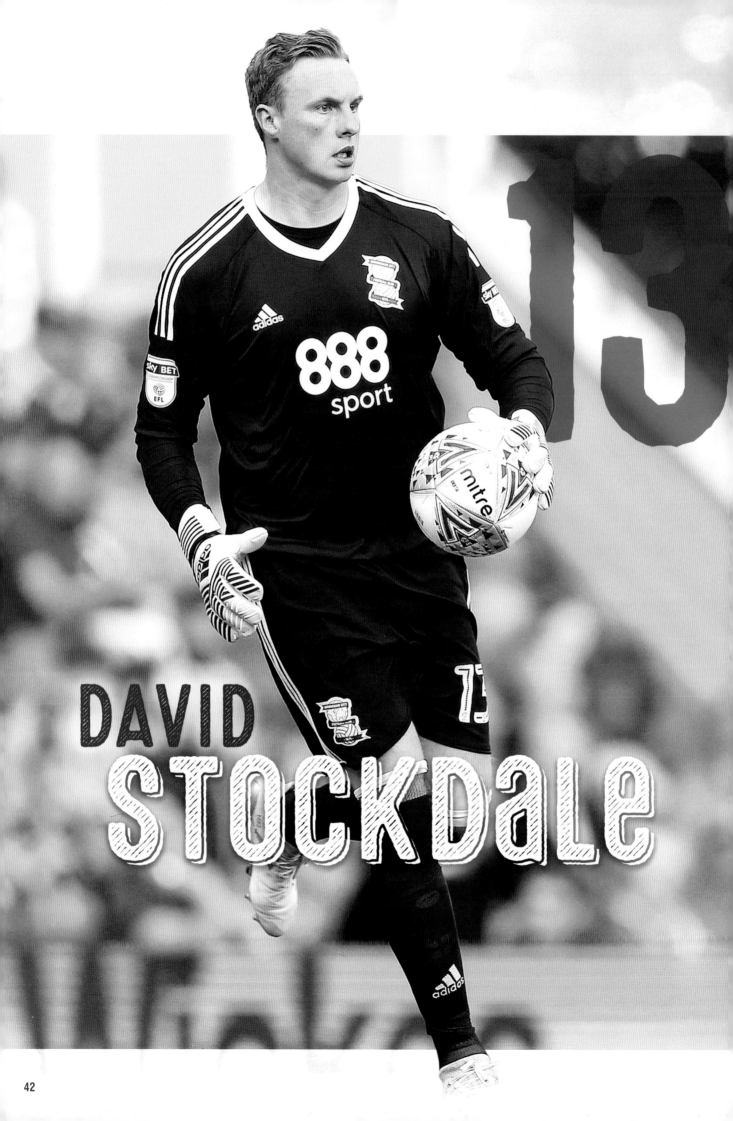

DAVID
STOCKDALE

DURING A SHORT BUT HIGHLY IMPACTFUL BLUES CAREER, CHRISTOPHE DUGARRY WON CULT STATUS AT ST. ANDREW'S AS HE INSPIRED THE CLUB TO PREMIER LEAGUE SURVIVAL IN 2002/03...

1. INSPIRATIONAL SIGNING

At the halfway stage of Blues' first season in the Premier League a bad start to 2003 had seen the team slip to 16th in the table and only five points separated them and 18th placed West Bromwich Albion. Boss Steve Bruce strengthened his squad with the January signings of Stephen Clemence, Jamie Clapham and Matthew Upson but his master stroke was taking French striker Christophe Dugarry on loan from Bordeaux.

2. WORLD CUP WINNER

When Dugarry arrived at St. Andrew's he already had World Cup and European Championship winning medals to his name having been involved with France's successes in 1998 and 2000. He became only the second World Cup winner to player for Blues - the first being Argentinian Alberto Tarantini. Dugarry oozed class on the pitch and his commitment to the cause won him the respect of fans and teammates alike.

3. CRUCIAL WIN

Despite Blues failing to register a win during Dugarry's first five games for the Club, it all came good at St. Andrew's on Sunday 23 February as Dugarry played a starring role in a crucial 2-1 victory over Liverpool. Goals from Stephen Clemence and Clinton Morrison sealed the win but it was Dugarry who received at standing ovation when he departed on 81 minutes to be replaced by Geoff Horsfield.

4. DERBY DELIGHT

The win over Liverpool sent Blues into the second city derby with Aston Villa full of confidence. Once again Dugarry starred and Blues won. Second-half goals from Stan Lazaridis and Geoff Horsfield secured a memorable win at Villa Park as Bruce's men completed a league double over their fiercest rivals.

5. AMONG THE GOALS

After helping inspire his teammates to vital victories with his performances, Dugarry then got among the goals himself as Blues climbed the table and secured Premier League status. His first goal for Blues came in a 2-0 victory over Sunderland at St. Andrew's in April and signalled a run of five goals in four games including a brace in a thrilling 3-2 home win against Southampton.

6. STAYING ON

After being recognised as the catalyst for Blues' successful battle against relegation while on loan, fans were keen for Dugarry to join on a permanent basis. He agreed a permanent two-year deal at St. Andrew's but was unable to rediscover the breathtaking form he showed during his initial loan spell. He left the Club by mutual consent in 2004 but few will forget his contribution and he has since been inducted into the Club's Hall of Fame.

CHRISTOPHE DUGARRY'S

SIX STEPS TO STARDOM

WORLD CUP

WHEN THE SEASON COMES TO AN END IN MAY, THE FOOTBALL DOESN'T STOP!

When Blues' campaign is over and the Championship prizes are handed out, you can sit back and get ready to watch the World's international superstars take to the pitch for the 2018 FIFA World Cup which starts on 14 June.

Just to get you in the mood, try this World Cup quiz!

1930

The first World Cup was won by the host nation Uruguay, but who did they defeat 4-2 in the final?

During England's first-ever World Cup in Brazil, they were beaten 1-0 by a team of part-timers from which country?

1966

Birmingham's mascot is Beau Brummie, but what was the name of the official World Cup mascot when England beat Germany 4-2 to win the World Cup?

1934

The host nation were victorious again! Italy beat Czechoslovakia 2-1, but do you know how many times the Italians have won the World Cup?

1954

Which country scored 27 goals, the most of the tournament? Ferenc Puskás netted four of them!

1970

Arguably the greatest World Cup final of all time was in 1970, when brilliant Brazil won 4-1. Who did they beat?

1938

Italy retained the trophy with a 4-2 victory over Hungary, in which European capital?

1958 & 1962

The same name went on the trophy in 1958 and 1962, the first and second of their record five wins. Who are they?

1974

The Dutch captain produced one of the World Cup's most iconic moments - a 180 degree wrong-footing turn that totally outwitted the defender. What is the move called?

QUIZ...

1978
Which former Blues star helped his home nation Argentina lift the World Cup in 1978?

1994
The record for most goals in a single match by one player is five, scored by Oleg Salenko as Cameroon were crushed 6-1 by which nation?

2006
Which former Blues fan favourite was part of Australia's squad that reached the last 16?

1982
Which Northern Ireland player became the youngest-ever, at 17 years, one month and 10 days old, to appear in the final stages of the World Cup?

1998
Who won the Golden Ball award for the tournament's best player?

2010
Only one country remained unbeaten throughout the whole tournament. Which nation was it?

1986
Which legendary Argentinian scored twice to knock England out at the quarter-final stage 2-1?

2002
This German star scored a hat-trick in the 8-0 demolition of Saudi Arabia - the first of his record 16 goals in World Cup finals. Who is he?

2014
Which country staged the last World Cup in 2014 and who are the World Cup holders?

1990
In the opening match, the holders Argentina suffered a shock 1-0 defeat to which African nation?

2018
Where are the World Cup finals going to be held next summer?

ANSWERS ON PAGE 62

The central defensive pairing of Scott Dann and Roger Johnson proved a pivotal cog in the Blues side that registered the Club's highest final league position in 50 years when Alex McLeish's team finished ninth in the Premier League in 2009/10.

DOUBLE

After winning promotion back to the Premier League at the first time of asking in 2008/09, McLeish was keen to bolster the strength of his squad ahead of the 2009/10 campaign. In a busy summer at St. Andrew's he recruited both Dann and Johnson in what proved to be two exceptionally shrewd pieces of business by the Blues boss.

Blues became Dann's third Midlands club when he joined on 12 June 2009 from Coventry City having begun his career with nearby Walsall. His arrival at St. Andrew's was described as a 'Club record fee for a defender' but injury delayed his debut and the commencement of his formidable partnership with Johnson.

Just 13 days after Dann's arrival, Johnson completed his move from Cardiff City to St. Andrew's and gave an impressive debut on the opening day of the season as Blues suffered a narrow 1-0 defeat to Manchester United.

JOHNSON

Johnson proved to the be the rock that McLeish built his back four around and such was his reliability, form and fitness that he was ever-present during his first season at St. Andrew's.

ACTS

& DANN

Dann meanwhile played in 30 Premier League games as the two players formed an excellent understanding at the heart of the defence that provided a level of confidence which subsequently flowed throughout the team.

After ensuring Blues recorded that impressive ninth place finish in their first season at the Club, the two defenders then played vital roles the following season as Blues enjoyed Wembley glory in the League Cup. Sadly for Dann he suffered a hamstring injury in the first leg of the semi-final against West Ham United and missed the Wembley victory over Arsenal. Such was the serious nature of the injury he was ruled out for the remainder of the season and his absence certainly proved costly as Blues were relegated on the final day of the campaign.

Unsurprisingly Dann and Johnson were courted by Premier League sides with their outstanding partnership in 2009/10 and the first half of 2010/11 still fresh in the minds of other clubs. Both players left St. Andrew's following relegation in the summer of 2011 - Johnson joined Midlands rivals Wolves while Dann headed north to try his luck with Blackburn Rovers.

Design their kit, add hair, be creative!

MaKe your own FOOZBaLL Team

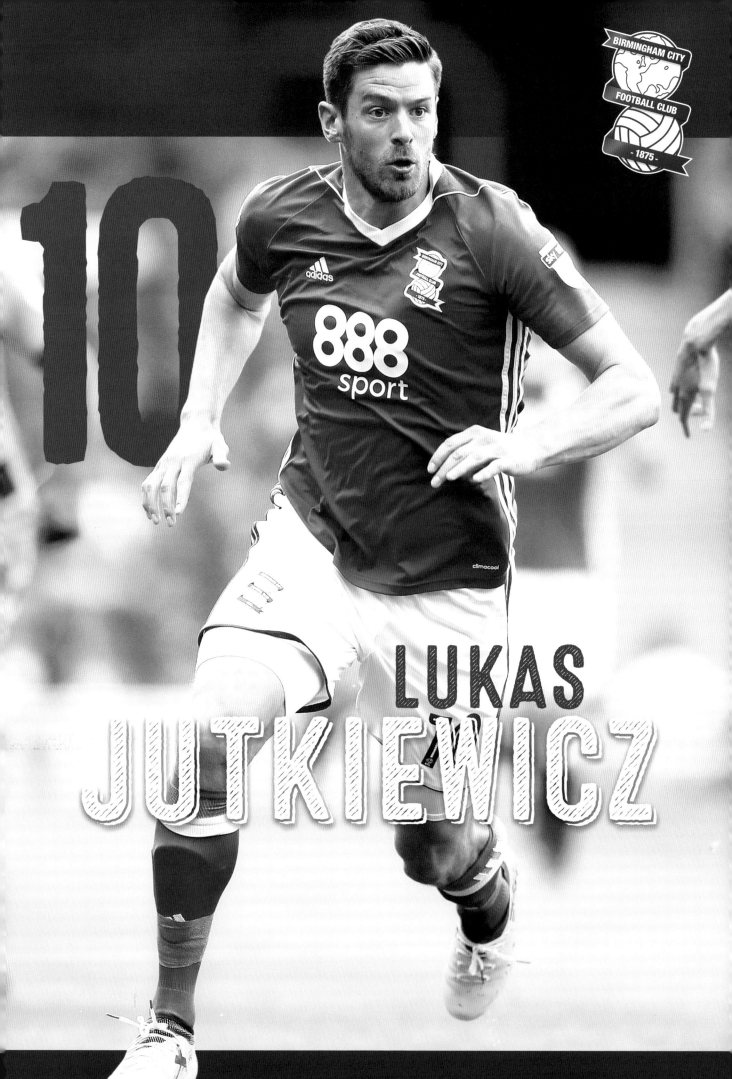

LUKAS
JUTKIEWICZ

There's something special about football over the festive period. With matches coming thick and fast, the points on offer can help shape a club's season. Blues have certainly enjoyed some festive cheer over the years - here are four to remember.

TEAM OF 1971/72

DECEMBER 27 1971

BIRMINGHAM CITY 3
CARDIFF CITY 0

After being held to three consecutive Second Division draws, Blues turned on the style to defeat Cardiff City 3-0 on 27 December during the Club's 1971/72 promotion-winning campaign.

A bumper festive crowd of 40,793 were inside St. Andrew's to see Freddie Goodwin's men run out comfortable winners with goals from Garry Pendrey, Bob Hatton and Trevor Francis ensuring the home fans went home happy.

This win was certainly a vital one and moved Blues up to fifth in the Second Division table. Goodwin's men eventually secured promotion as runner-ups to Norwich City on the final day of the season.

CHRISTMAS

STEVE CLARIDGE

STEVE McGAVIN IN ACTION AGAINST CAMBRIDGE UNITED

DECEMBER 3 1994

BIRMINGHAM CITY 7
BLACKPOOL 1

Blues ended the calendar year of 1994 in the best possible way as they followed up a Boxing Day draw with Cambridge United and a narrow 1-0 win away to Cardiff City with a 7-1 thrashing of Blackpool at St. Andrew's.

Under the management of Barry Fry this resounding triumph took Blues to the top of Division Two as the Club looked to return to the Division One at the first time of asking.

Leading scorer Steve Claridge netted a brace as did winger Louie Donowa. Kenny Lowe and George Parris were also on target with Blackpool defender Darren Bradshaw adding his name to the scoresheet with an own goal. With goalscoring prowess like this it was unsurprising that Blues ended the season as Division Two champions.

GEOFF HORSFIELD

DECEMBER 26 2001

SHEFFIELD WEDNESDAY 0
BIRMINGHAM CITY 1

Geoff Horsfield was Blues' Boxing Day hero as he netted the only goal of the game at Hillsborough to secure three vital points during the Club's memorable 2001/02 Nationwide First Division campaign.

Blues had enjoyed a narrow 1-0 win at home to Midlands rivals Walsall three days before Christmas and this Boxing Day triumph over Sheffield Wednesday was followed by a 3-0 win at Stockport County that propelled them into the play-off places as the team continued to gain momentum under new manager Steve Bruce.

This classic campaign ended with Birmingham winning promotion to the Premier League following a penalty shoot-out victory over Norwich City in the play-off final.

CRACKERS

BIRMINGHAM CITY 3
MIDDLESBROUGH 0

DECEMBER 26 2007

Birmingham registered their first home win under the management of Alex McLeish as they eased past Boro on Boxing Day 2007 to give the St. Andrew's crowd some festive cheer in what was a frustrating campaign for the Club.

A Stewart Downing own-goal gave Blues the perfect start and Mikael Forssell doubled the lead before the break. Gary McSheffrey successfully converted a second-half penalty to extinguish any hopes of a Boro revival and wrapped up the points.

This was Blues' last top-flight Boxing Day win but sadly was not enough to prevent relegation at the end of the 2007/08 campaign.

GARY McSHEFFREY IN ACTION AGAINST MIDDLESBROUGH

51

Jaap Stam   **Steve Bruce**   **Mick McCarthy**

FANTASTIC

emilio
NSUE
2

54

NATHAN REDMOND

Born in Birmingham on 6 March 1994, flying winger Nathan Redmond progressed from Blues' Academy to first team favourite and has since gone on to enjoy Premier League stardom.

After consistently impressing at Academy level, often performing at a higher age group, Redmond made his first team debut in a League Cup tie against Rochdale in August 2010 as a 78th minute replacement for Enric Valles. He was aged just 16 years and 173 days old and became the second youngest player to represent Birmingham City.

The 2010/11 season saw him make two further substitute appearances and his progress was rewarded with a three-year professional contract just as soon as he turned 17.

Chris Hughton had great faith in Redmond's talent and handed him the chance to shine on a regular basis in the 2011/12 season. A local boy with electric pace and an eye for goal - Redmond had the lot and scored a memorable first goal for the Club in the 3-0 Europa League play-off match against Nacional as Blues progressed to the group stage.

In total Redmond made 82 appearances for Blues, scoring nine goals and also gaining his first England U21 caps while at St. Andrew's. His scintillating displays that made such a popular figure with Blues' fans had also caught the eye of the outside world and in the summer of 2013 he opted to showcase his talents at Premier League level. Redmond joined Norwich City and linked up again with former Blues boss Hughton who had taken over at Carrow Road in 2012.

Redmond was a great success at Norwich and despite the Canaries' relegation in 2014 he remained at Carrow Road and was a key player in their promotion back to the Premier League via the play-offs in 2014/15 with goals in both the semi-final and Wembley final.

After Norwich suffered relegation for a second time in three seasons, Redmond opted to remain in the Premier League and secured a reported £10m move to Southampton in June 2016.

His career has continued to blossom at St Mary's and he won his first full England cap in March 2017 during England's friendly with Germany.

MADE IN BIRMINGHAM

You'd definitely recognise St. Andrew's but can you figure out which football clubs these grounds belong to...

Home Turf

1

2

Team:

Ground:

Capacity:

3

Team:

Ground:

Capacity:

4

Team:

Ground:

Capacity:

Team:

Ground:

Capacity:

5

6

Team:

Ground:

Capacity:

Team:

Ground:

Capacity:

Team:

Ground:

Capacity:

AST STAND

7

8

Team:

Ground:

Capacity:

10

Team:

Ground:

Capacity:

Team:

Ground:

Capacity:

9

ANSWERS ON PAGE 62

11

...as well as their official name and capacity?!

12

13

14

Team: _____
Ground: _____
Capacity: _____

Team: _____
Ground: _____
Capacity: _____

Team: _____
Ground: _____
Capacity: _____

Team: _____
Ground: _____
Capacity: _____

15

16

Team: _____
Ground: _____
Capacity: _____

Team: _____
Ground: _____
Capacity: _____

17

18

19

Team: _____
Ground: _____
Capacity: _____

Team: _____
Ground: _____
Capacity: _____

20

Team: _____
Ground: _____
Capacity: _____

Team: _____
Ground: _____
Capacity: _____

Five games to watch out for...

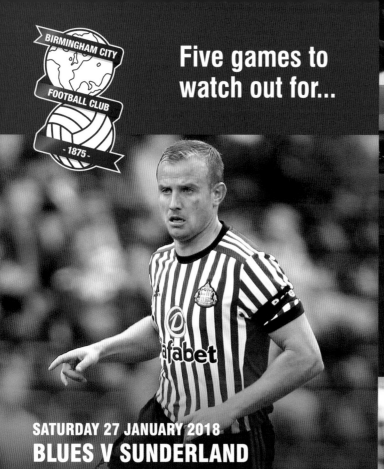

SATURDAY 27 JANUARY 2018
BLUES V SUNDERLAND

Having been relegated from the Premier League at the end of the 2016/17 campaign, Sunderland visit St. Andrew's on the last weekend of January. Amongst their ranks, Simon Grayson's side includes former Blues favourite Seb Larsson, who was part of the side that won the 2011 Carling Cup with Blues and was part of the 2006/07 and part of the 2008/09 promotion-winning sides. The Black Cats will be looking to bounce back into the top flight at the first time of asking.

SUNDAY 11 FEBRUARY 2018
ASTON VILLA V BLUES

Any game against Blues' biggest rivals barely needs an introduction. Expect passion, fierce challenges and an electrically charged atmosphere as Blues make the short trip to Aston. Blues will be looking for a first victory at the home of the old enemy since a 2-1 Premiership success in December 2004. But this time, with Harry Redknapp at the helm, the chances of Blues upsetting the Villans on their home soil is better than it has been for a long time.

SATURDAY 17 FEBRUARY 2018
BLUES V MILLWALL

Blues entertain the Lions at St. Andrew's in mid-February. Millwall will be looking to consolidate their place in the Championship having won promotion at the end of the 2016/17 season after beating Bradford City in the League One play-off final at Wembley. Blues of course have play-off history of their own against the Lions after beating them in the Championship play-off semi-final in 2001/02, something that the South Londoners have never forgotten.

SUNDAY 15 APRIL 2018
WOLVES V BLUES

Blues are unbeaten in their last three trips to the home of their Midland rivals Wolverhampton Wanderers and they will be looking to maintain that recent record at Molineux. Nuno Espírito Santo was appointed as Wolves' Head Coach at the end of May 2017 and the former Portugal U21 goalkeeper has brought in several of his compatriots as he attempts to lead Wolves to promotion.

SUNDAY 6 MAY 2018
BLUES V FULHAM

Blues' final game of the 2017/18 season sees them play host to the Cottagers at St. Andrew's. Managed by ex-Yugoslavia internal Slaviša Jokanovi, Fulham have every chance of challenging towards the top of the table with the players they have at their disposal. Amongst their squad they also count former Blues Academy graduate Sone Aluko.

JANUARY 2018

Tuesday	2	Reading	A	8.00pm
Saturday	**13**	**Derby County**	**H**	**3.00pm**
Saturday	20	Preston North End	A	3.00pm
Saturday	**27**	**Sunderland**	**H**	**3.00pm**

FEBRUARY 2018

Saturday	3	Sheffield Wed	A	3.00pm
Saturday	11	Aston Villa	A	12 noon
Saturday	**17**	**Millwall**	**H**	**3.00pm**
Tuesday	20	Brentford	A	7.45pm
Saturday	**24**	**Barnsley**	**H**	**3.00pm**

MARCH 2018

Saturday	3	Nottingham Forest	A	3.00pm
Tuesday	**6**	**Middlesbrough**	**H**	**7.45pm**
Saturday	10	Cardiff City	A	3.00pm
Saturday	**17**	**Hull City**	**H**	**3.00pm**
Saturday	**31**	**Ipswich Town**	**H**	**3.00pm**

APRIL 2018

Tuesday	3	Bolton Wanderers	A	8.00pm
Saturday	**7**	**Burton Albion**	**H**	**3.00pm**
Tuesday	10	Bristol City	A	7.45pm
Sunday	15	Wolves	A	1.00pm
Saturday	**21**	**Sheffield United**	**H**	**3.00pm**
Saturday	28	QPR	A	3.00pm

MAY 2018

Sunday	**6**	**Fulham**	**H**	**12.30pm**

JOSH DACRES-COGLEY

The 2016/17 Sky Bet Championship season certainly proved to be a breakthrough campaign for 21-year-old full-back Josh Dacres-Cogley whose impressive performances were recognised with a new three-year contract.

Despite Blues having the upheaval of three managers in one season, the former Academy scholar clearly impressed each of Gary Rowett, Gianfranco Zola and Harry Redknapp during a season of rapid rise for the popular right-back.

Schooled in Warwick, Dacres-Cogley initially joined Blues' Academy in 2011 and was handed a scholarship a year later. With energy and pace to burn, coupled with a desire to get forward and support the attack at any given opportunity, Dacres-Cogley has all the attributes a manager would look for in the modern day full-back.

MADE IN BIRMINGHAM

He was handed his first team debut by Rowett in Blues' EFL Cup tie at home to Oxford United on 9 August and a league debut arrived in November. Although Blues bowed out of the EFL Cup 1-0 to Oxford, Dacres-Cogley's league debut at Brentford proved a happier affair as he played a starring role in a hard-fought 2-1 victory at Griffin Park. His performance won him the praise of his manager who passed public comment on the youngster's energy, composure and athleticism.

In total Dacres-Cogley made 17 appearances for Blues last season as the Club maintained their Championship status in dramatic style. Now with an exciting new era on the horizon under new boss Redknapp, the future looks bright for Birmingham City and this young man in particular.

Time will tell if Dacres-Cogley's talents will be developed further by Redknapp in Blues' 2017/18 squad or if he will be offered the opportunity to gain valuable experience on loan. Whatever the next 12 months hold, his future is committed to Birmingham City and the Club clearly have another promising home grown talent on their hands.

MARC
ROBERTS

4

ANSWERS

PAGE 26 · WHO ARE YA?

1. David Cotterill, 2. Lukas Jutkiewicz, 3. Isaac Vassell, 4. Marc Roberts,
5. Josh Dacres-Cogley, 6. Paul Robinson, 7. Che Adams,
8. Corey O'Keeffe, 9. Jonathan Grounds, 10. Wes Harding.

PAGE 31 · FOOTBALL 50

Fixture

PAGE 35 · WHAT BALL?

Picture A - Ball 3, Picture B - Ball 8.

PAGE 38
CHAMPIONSHIP CHALLENGE PART 1

1. John Terry, 2. Bayern Munich, 3. Steve Bruce, 4. Angus MacDonald,
5. Crystal Palace, 6. Paul Heckingbottom, 7. Craig Gardner, 8. 2011,
9. Jota, 10. Four times, 11. Middlesbrough, 12. Phil Parkinson,
13. 4-1, 14. Neal Maupay, 15. Mark Warburton, 16. Tammy Abraham,
17. Watford, 18. Tammy Abraham, 19. Nigel Clough, 20. Liam Boyce,
21. Stephen Warnock, 22. Red, 23. Neil Warnock, 24. Gary Medel,
25. Bradley Johnson, 26. 1946, 27. Tom Huddlestone, 28. Atletico Madrid,
29. Marcus Bettinelli, 30. Tom Cairney, 31. The Tigers, 32. Russia,
33. Arsenal, 34. Joe Garner, 35. Sir Alf Ramsey, 36. 1977/78.

PAGE 40
CHAMPIONSHIP CHALLENGE PART 2

37. Marching On Together, 38. Seven, 39. Liam Cooper,
40. Connor Roberts, 41. Seville, 42. The League Cup, 43. Neil Harris,
44. Manchester United, 45. The Lions, 46. Borussia Dortmund II, 47. Four,
48. Angus Gunn, 49. Newcastle United, 50. True, 51. Liam Bridcutt,
52. Jordan Hugill, 53. David Moyes, 54. Won all four divisions of English
football, 55. Nedum Onuoha, 56. Christopher Samba, 57. Martin O'Neill,
58. Jaap Stam, 59. Third, 60. Vito Mannone, 61. Leon Clarke, 62. 100,
63. Chelsea, 64. George Boyd, 65. 150 years old, they were formed in 1867,
66. 8, 67. Callum McManaman, 68. Three: Aston Villa, Preston North End
and Leeds United, 69. George Honeyman and Lynden Gooch,
70. Southampton, 71. Six, 72. Ruben Neves.

PAGE 44 · WORLD CUP QUIZ

1930 - Argentina, 1934 - Four, 1938 - Paris, 1950 - USA, 1954 - Hungary,
1958 & 1962 - Brazil, 1966 - World Cup Willie, 1970 - Italy,
1974 - The Cruyff turn, after legendary Dutch footballer Johan Cruyff,
1978 - Alberto Tarantini, 1982 - Norman Whiteside v Yugoslavia, 0-0, 17
June 1982, 1986 - Diego Maradona, 1990 - Cameroon, 1994 - Russia,
1998 - Ronaldo, 2002 - Miroslav Klose, 2006 - Stan Lazaridis,
2010 - New Zealand. They drew all three of the games,
2014 - Hosts: Brazil. Winners: Germany, 2018 - Russia.

PAGE 52 · FANTASTIC

PAGE 56 · HOME TURF

1. West Bromwich Albion, The Hawthorns, 26,852
2. Burnley, Turf Moor, 21,800
3. Everton, Goodison Park, 39,572
4. Arsenal, Emirates Stadium, 60,432
5. Manchester United, Old Trafford, 75,643
6. Aston Villa, Villa Park, 42,682
7. Queens Park Rangers, Loftus Road, 18,439
8. Sunderland, Stadium of Light, 49,000
9. Ipswich Town, Portman Road, 30,311
10. Nottingham Forest, City Ground, 30,445
11. West Ham United, London Stadium, 57,000
12. Fulham, Craven Cottage, 25,700
13. Leicester City, King Power Stadium, 32,312
14. Southampton, St Mary's Stadium, 32,505
15. Stoke City, bet365 Stadium, 27,902
16. Norwich City, Carrow Road, 27,244
17. Wolverhampton Wanderers, Molineux Stadium, 31,700
18. Millwall, The Den, 20,146
19. Chelsea, Stamford Bridge, 41,663
20. Derby County, Pride Park Stadium, 33,597